FOR LISA THOMSON,
MY BFF IN HIGH SCHOOL AND HAPPILY EVER AFTER

Graphic Universe™
A division of Lerner Publishing Group, Inc.
241 First Avenue North
Minneapolis, MN 55401 USA

For reading levels and more information, look up this title at www.lernerbooks.com.

Library of Congress Cataloging-in-Publication Data

Names: MariNaomi, author, illustrator.
Title: Losing the girl / by MariNaomi.
Description: Minneapolis : Graphic Universe, [2018] | Series: Life on Earth ; book 1 | Summary: As Blithedale searches for a missing girl, rumored to be abducted by aliens, a group of high school students experiences a series of romantic relationships and their effects on friendships.
Identifiers: LCCN 2017006225 (print) | LCCN 2017033504 (ebook) | ISBN 9781512498578 (eb pdf) | ISBN 9781512449105 (lb : alk. paper)
Subjects: LCSH: Graphic novels. | CYAC: Graphic novels. | Dating (Social customs)—Fiction. | Friendship—Fiction. | Missing children—Fiction. | Alien abduction—Fiction.
Classification: LCC PZ7.7.M339 (ebook) | LCC PZ7.7.M339 Los 2018 (print) | DDC [Fic]—dc23

LC record available at https://lccn.loc.gov/2017006225

Manufactured in the United States of America
1-42842-26506-5/17/2017

LIFE ON EARTH · BOOK 1

LOSING THE GIRL

MARINAOMI

Graphic Universe™ · Minneapolis

PART ONE

Nigel Jones

14

They were supposed to be together forever, but apparently all those movies and love songs lie.

27

30

YES!

36

An ollie!
Perfectly executed.

39

LIFE SUCKS!
How's that for "real"?

Um, that's a good start...

Like my dad is so PATHETIC.

He has some stupid "mid-life crisis," and the next thing you know, my mom kicks him out of the house.

41

43

46

There's no way Emily's gonna wait for me.

It's too long, a whole summer.

Ugh.

Shut up.

Shut up.

60

61

PART TWO

Emily Hiroko Baker

65

I can almost smell summer vacation.

The scent of freedom.

93

Mikhail B... the dancer?

Uh, I... think so?

In the 1920s he wrote a book, "Heart of a Dog."

It's about a stray mutt that gets surgically turned into a man.

It's symbolic of the trappings of a classist society.

Uh-huh ...

Uh, what??

So it's like, um, Frankenstein meets the Werewolf?

stupid
stupid
stupid
stupid
stupid

stupid
stupid

Not exactly.

117

119

130

135

emily? are you okay? emily?!

How freaky to think there's a little creature floating inside my belly.

Part of me wants to get it the hell out of me.

I mean, how creepy! A little parasite!

But...I also want to be a mom...someday.

I always thought I would be, just not so soon.

How can you plan these things?

150

What am I doing here?

I can't pretend everything's all right.

I've got to go.

I...need some space...

155

157

165

168

PART THREE

Brett Hathaway

She is so stubborn.

Perhaps she always will be.

Only three skips.
I'm losing my touch.

208

212

213

PART FOUR

Paula Navarro

It's not that I don't care for him.

You've got to believe me.

Of course I do.
I just can't let him
treat me bad anymore.

There's nothing
going on between me
and Brett.

I've seen how
his parents are.

Please, Darren.

His mom is so
passive-aggressive.

It's the last thing I ever want to be.

She doesn't seem to have the ability to
say what she wants
so she just throws around
GUILT like it's her
only defense.

225

I think I was born with a sense for when trouble is coming.

Emily can't possibly understand me.

She has no idea why I shouldn't be with Darren.

Doesn't she see the way he talks to me?

Maybe she just doesn't notice anything beyond herself.

GUILT

Tch tch tch.

How are you doing, little guy?

I can't believe it was so simple to cut an integral person from my life.

I did it, just like that.

It was the right thing to do, wasn't it?
I can barely look her in the eyes.

GUILT

If she ever
found out
she'd be

D
E
V
A
S
T
A
T
E D.

It would
ruin her.

243

That girl looks just like...

252

253

PART FIVE

Nigel Jones

257

258

263

264

The end...
for now.

ACKNOWLEDGMENTS

Thank you so much to the folks responsible for making this book happen, especially my editor Greg Hunter, my agent Gordon Warnock, and cover designer Lindsey Owens. Big love to my literary and personal cheerleaders Fiona Taylor (whose lovely mountain abode housed me as I put the finishing touches on this book), Lisa Thomson, Rob Kirby, Tom Neely, Craig Thompson, Amelie Sukiennik, Lainie Baker, and Christopher Pappalardo. Thanks to my writing and drawing mates for keeping me from going crazy during my long work days, particularly Yumi Sakugawa, Nicky Sa-Eun Schildkraut, Steph Cha, Amelia Gray, Hope Larson, and Jen Wang. Shout out to my online family, especially the Olds, Her-Moans, and WoC. Most of all, big thanks for the support of my real-life family: Mom and Dad, Sabrina and Greg, Sue Lake, and most of all Gary and the menagerie. I love you all.

ABOUT THE AUTHOR

MariNaomi is the award-winning author and illustrator of four comics memoirs. *Losing the Girl* is her first graphic novel and her first foray into fiction that (possibly) involves alien life-forms. She's also the creator of the Cartoonists of Color and Queer Cartoonists databases. She lives in California with her husband and many cats and dogs. Visit her at marinaomi.com or @marinaomi.

LIFE ON EARTH · BOOK 2

COMING IN 2019